W9-ARV-706

THE AVENGERS™

AN ORIGIN STORY

Based on the Marvel comic book series The Avengers
Adapted by Rich Thomas Jr.
Illustrated by Pat Olliffe *and* Hi-Fi Design

New York

marvelkids.com

TM & © 2013 Marvel & Subs.

Published by Marvel Press, an imprint of Disney Book Group. No part of this book may be reproduced or transmitted in any form or by any means, electronic or mechanical, including photocopying, recording, or by any information storage and retrieval system, without written permission from the publisher. For information address Marvel Press, 114 Fifth Avenue, New York, New York 10011-5690.

Case Illustrated by Pat Olliffe and Brian Miller
Designed by Jason Wojtowicz

Printed in the United States of America
Second Edition
1 3 5 7 9 10 8 6 4 2
G942-9090-6-13015
ISBN 978-1-4231-8308-2

SUSTAINABLE FORESTRY INITIATIVE Certified Sourcing
www.sfiprogram.org
SFI-00993
For Text Only

Like many great stories,

ours begins with a
troublemaker.

This one was named **Loki.** He lived in a place called Asgard with his brother, **Thor**, and their father, **Odin**, the king of the Realm. All of them had **powers** you and I could hardly dream of.

Even though Loki and Thor were both princes, Thor was first in line to be the next king of Asgard. This made Loki very **jealous.** He thought **he** should be king.

Loki used his wits to try and get Thor
into trouble so he could take his place
as king.

But Thor was clever and knew what his brother was
up to. As much as he hated to do it, Thor asked Odin's
permission to keep Loki prisoner on the **Isle of Silence**
so he would stop causing trouble.

Loki was furious. Not only was Thor set to be king, but now Loki could do nothing to stop him. Thor had used his strength to crush his brother.

But Loki had gifts, too. Among them was the power to make people see things that weren't really there. He could also send his spirit places his body could not go.

Then Loki had an idea.

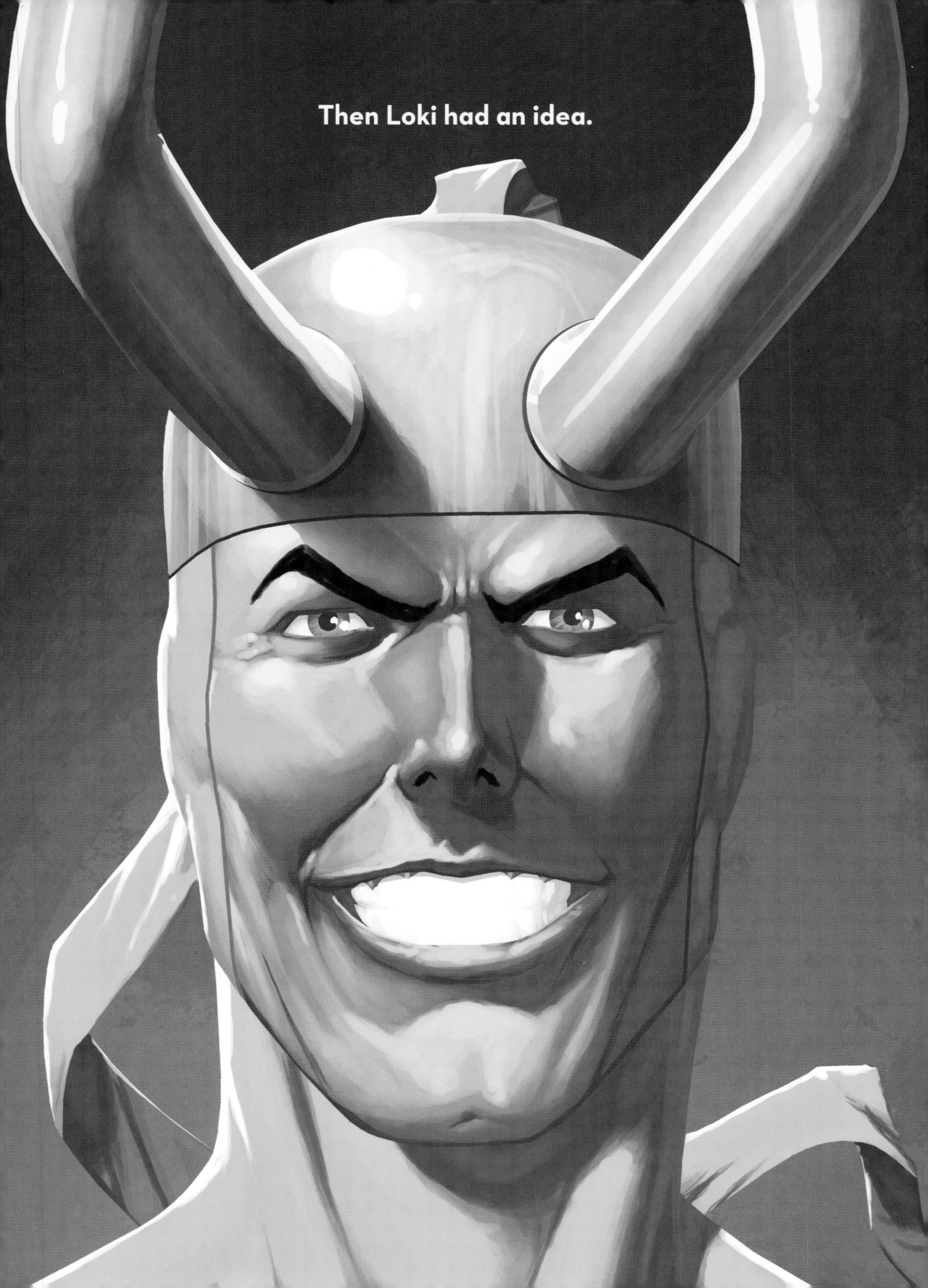

Loki knew that Thor spent most of his time on
Earth, disguised as a doctor named DON BLAKE.
And the Earth was filled with heroes.

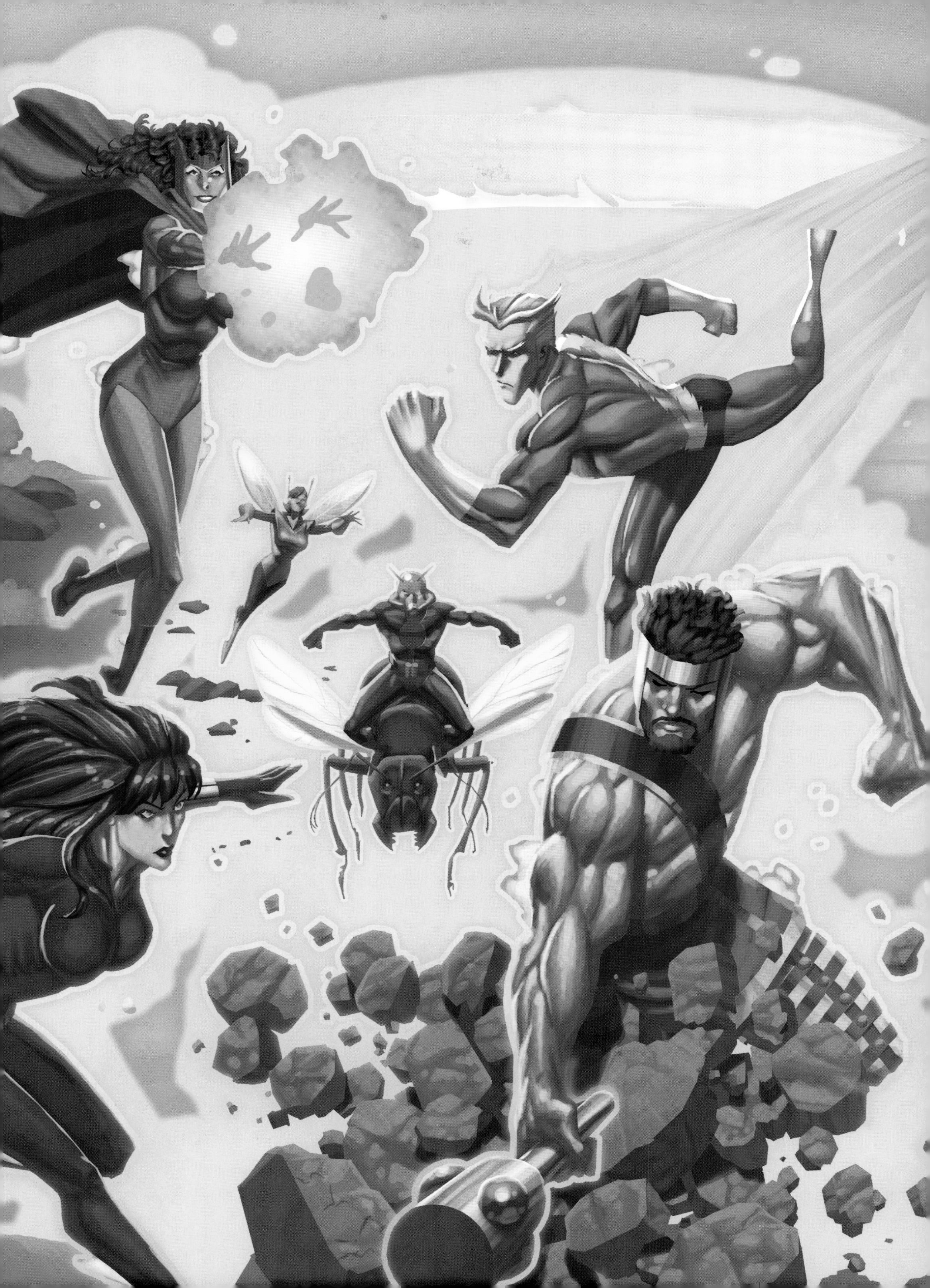

If Loki could find one that the people
of Earth didn't **trust**—

one who was **strong enough** to win a battle
with someone as powerful as Thor—

he could defeat his brother and
claim his place as next in line
to the throne of Asgard.

So Loki closed his eyes

and sent his spirit to Earth to find
the giant green hero, the **Hulk.**

Loki found the Hulk alone, far from any city.
He wasted no time putting his plan into action.

He used his powers to make it
appear that a nearby stretch
of railway tracks was **torn up.**
Just as Loki wanted, the Hulk
quickly noticed—

and jumped on the tracks to
stop the train from crashing.

But the people on the train thought the Hulk was trying to hurt them, not help them.

So the Hulk jumped away from the scene.

This is just what Loki had wanted. Thor was sure to try to stop the Hulk. And the Hulk would defeat Thor!

As the news quickly made its way across the country, it caught the attention of **DON BLAKE**—just as Loki thought it would.

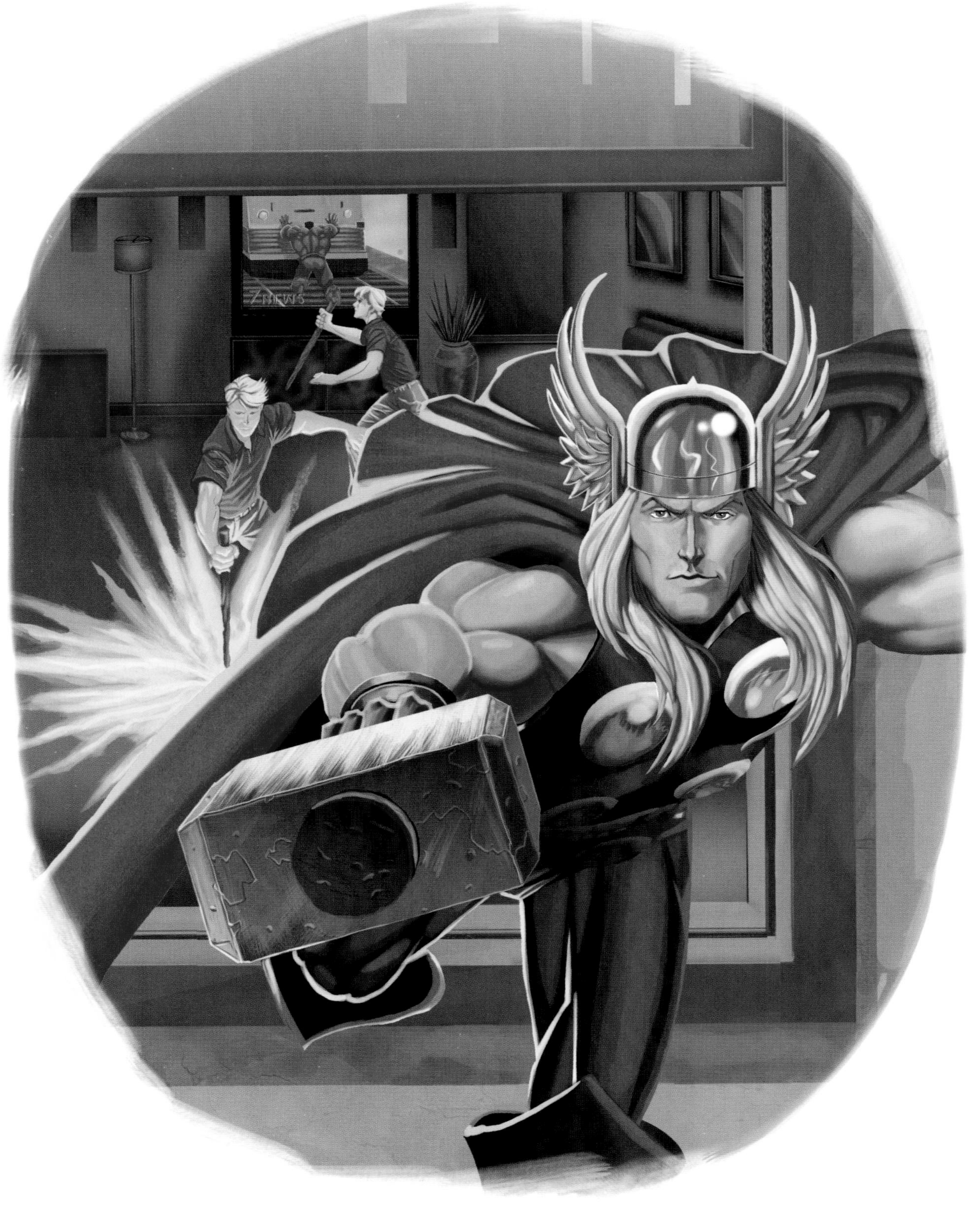

And at nearby Stark Industries Tower, billionaire **TONY STARK** also heard what the Hulk had been up to. He quickly suited up as **Iron Man** and rushed to the scene.

In a high-rise lab in New York City, **Dr. Henry Pym** and **Janet Van Dyne** also heard the alert . . .

and changed into
the Super Heroes

Ant-Man and
Wasp.

They rushed off to find the
Hulk and save the day.

All the heroes arrived at the same time. The police were happy to see so many of them in one place. Even the **Hulk** would have trouble stopping **four** Super Heroes.

But someone else wasn't so happy. Loki wanted the Hulk to fight only Thor. He needed to get Thor **away** from the others.

Loki created an image that only Thor could see.

The Mighty Thor cornered what he thought was the Hulk in a vacant lot.

Thor launched his hammer . . .

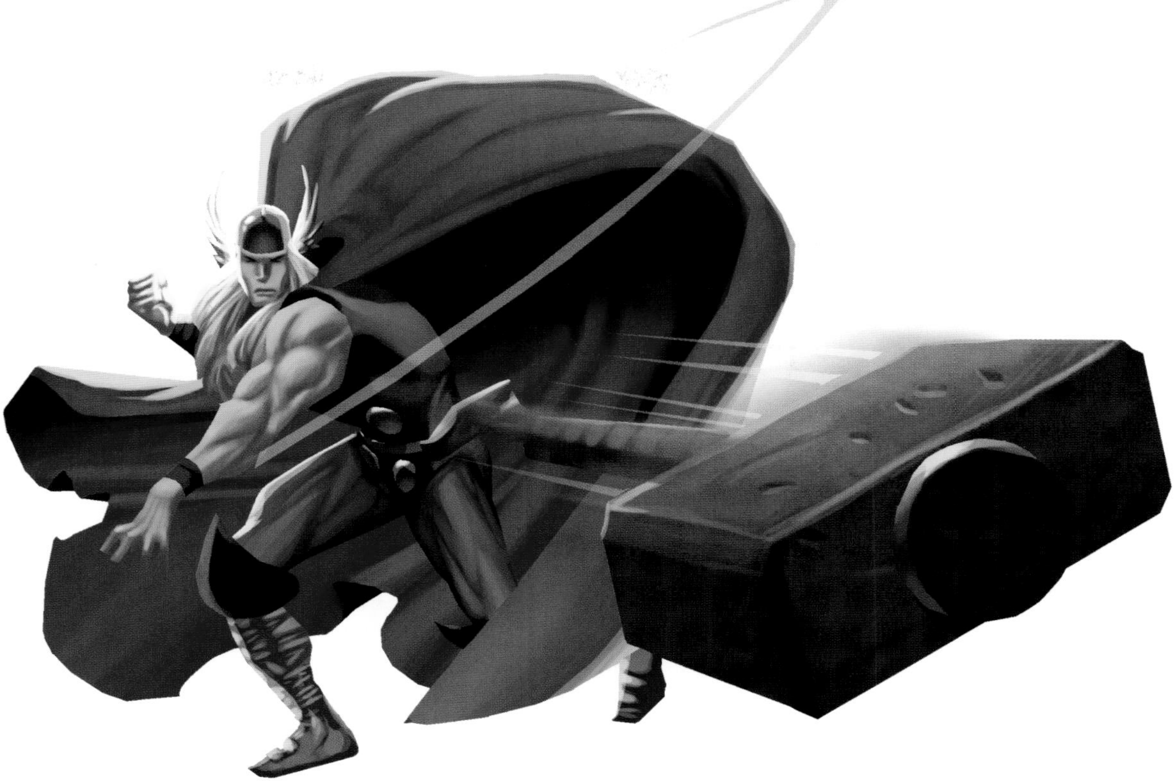

and that's when he realized his brother was up to his **old tricks.**

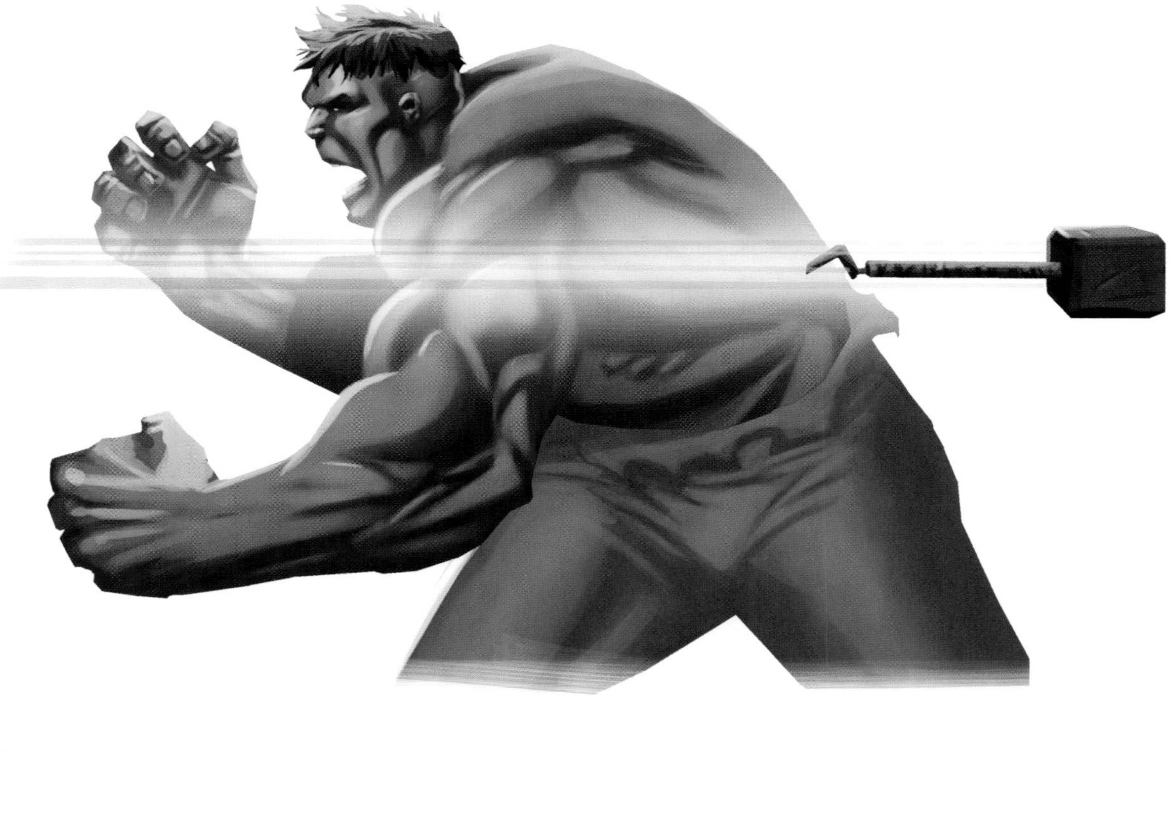

Only Loki could work magic like this. Thor now knew that the Hulk was **not** to blame. He flew off toward Asgard to stop Loki and set things right. The others were confused by Thor's leaving. They still thought the Hulk needed to be stopped.

Just then, a **swarm of ants** signaled to Ant-Man
that they had found the **real** Hulk.

Ant-Man told Iron Man and Wasp
to follow them!

The Super Heroes tracked the Hulk to a nearby circus.

The Hulk saw the heroes and quickly
disguised himself as a circus performer.

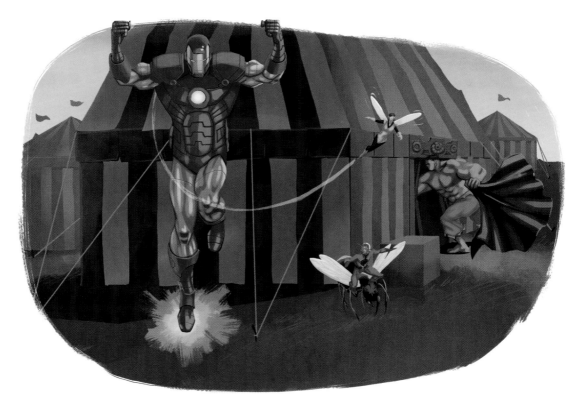

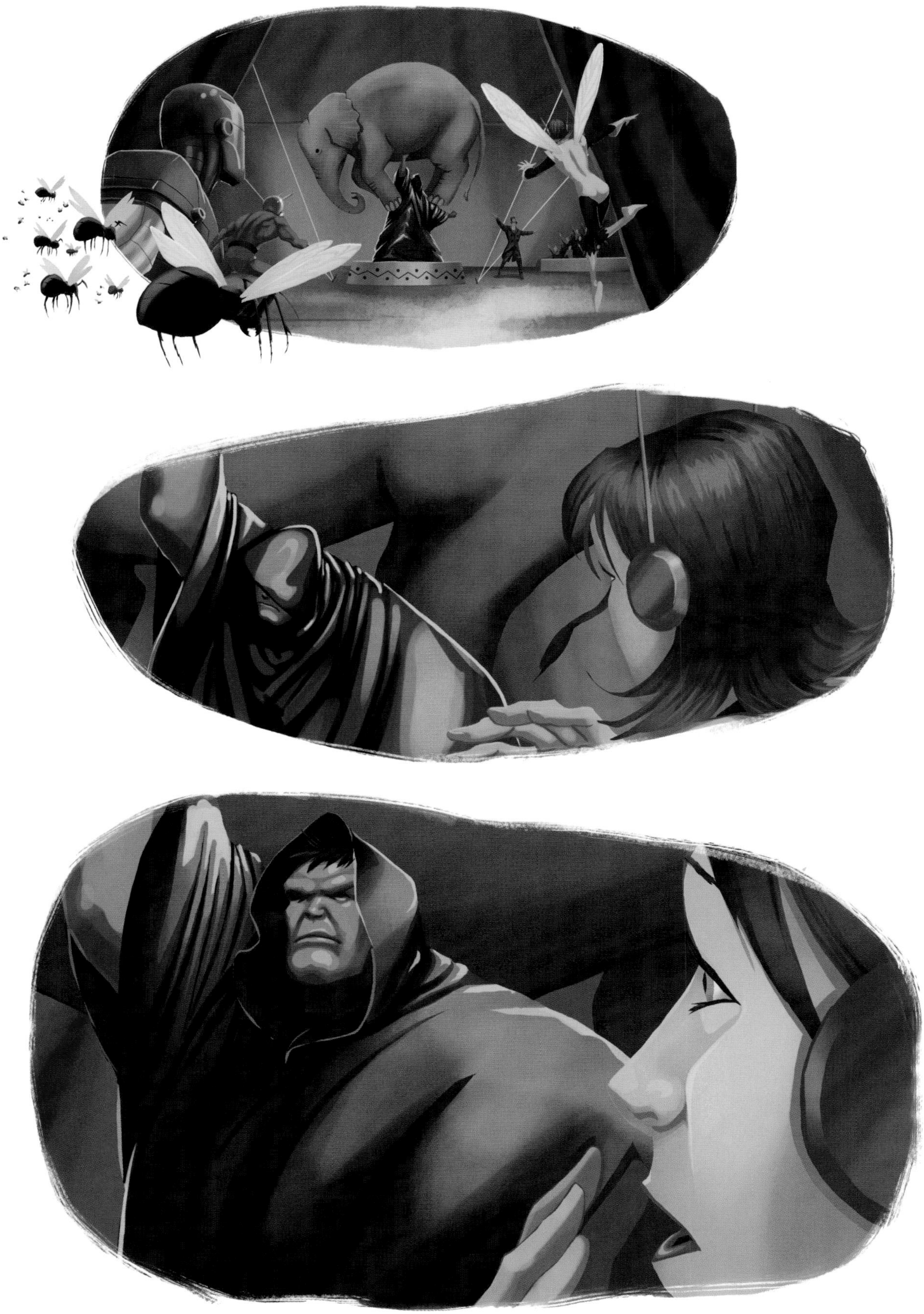

The heroes still thought the Hulk was **dangerous**,
so Ant-Man and Wasp attacked him . . .

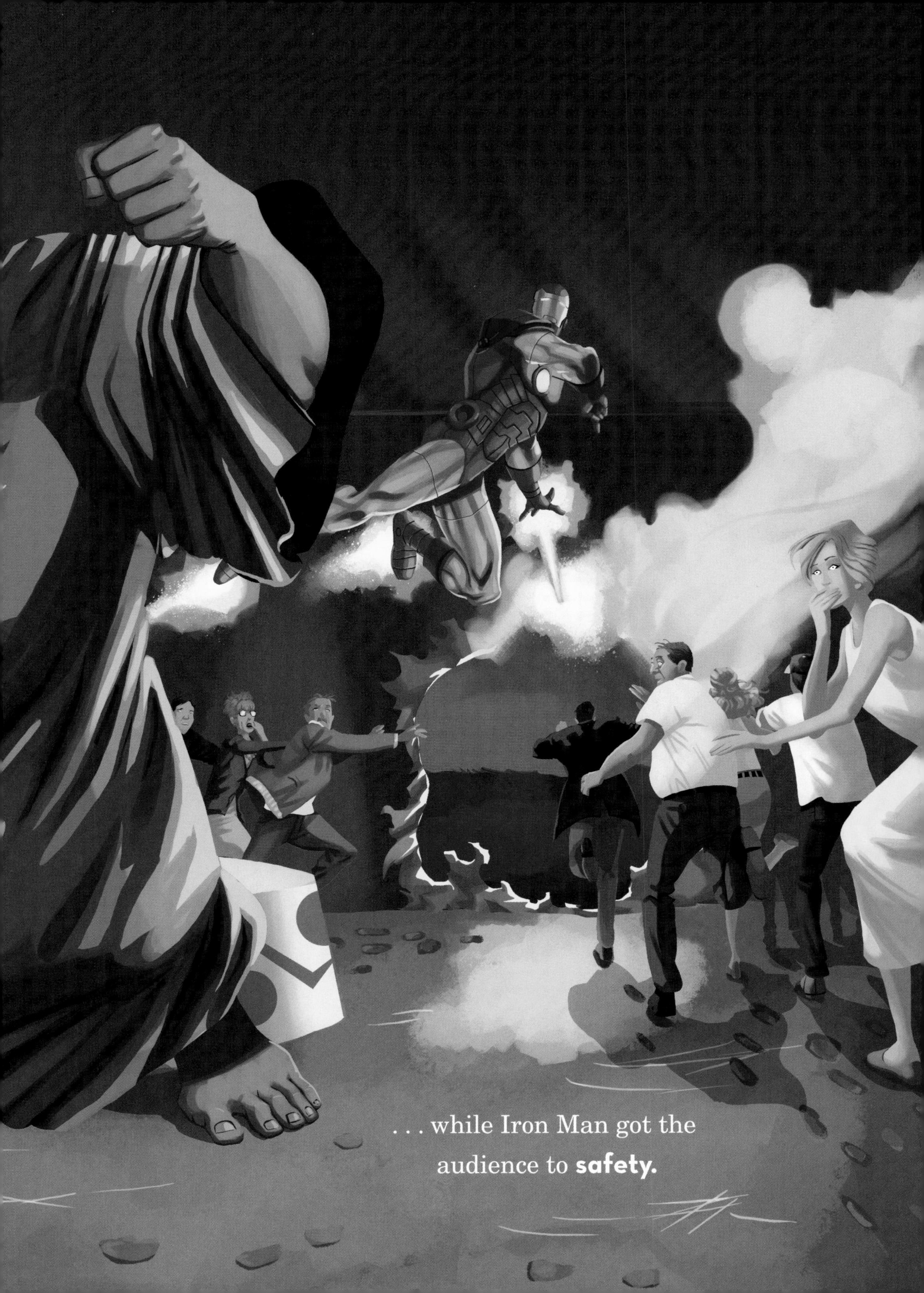

. . . while Iron Man got the
audience to **safety.**

Once Iron Man had cleared the area,
he joined the fight.

And as the battle raged on, **another** was about to begin.

Thor raced over the Bifrost
as fast as he could.

He quickly arrived at the **Isle of Silence** to bring the **real** threat to justice!

But Loki had been expecting his brother.

Loki called upon the **Silent Ones**—
Trolls who lived belowground on the isle.

The Silent Ones attacked Thor and pulled him underground.

But Thor was **not** so easily beaten.

Thor defeated the Silent Ones,
but in the struggle, **Loki escaped!**

Thor quickly went after his brother.

He found him at the Bifrost, which linked Asgard to other realms. Loki had created an **illusion** to distract **Heimdall**, the Asgardian who guarded the bridge, and sneaked past.

But even though Heimdall hadn't seen the real Loki, **Thor** had.

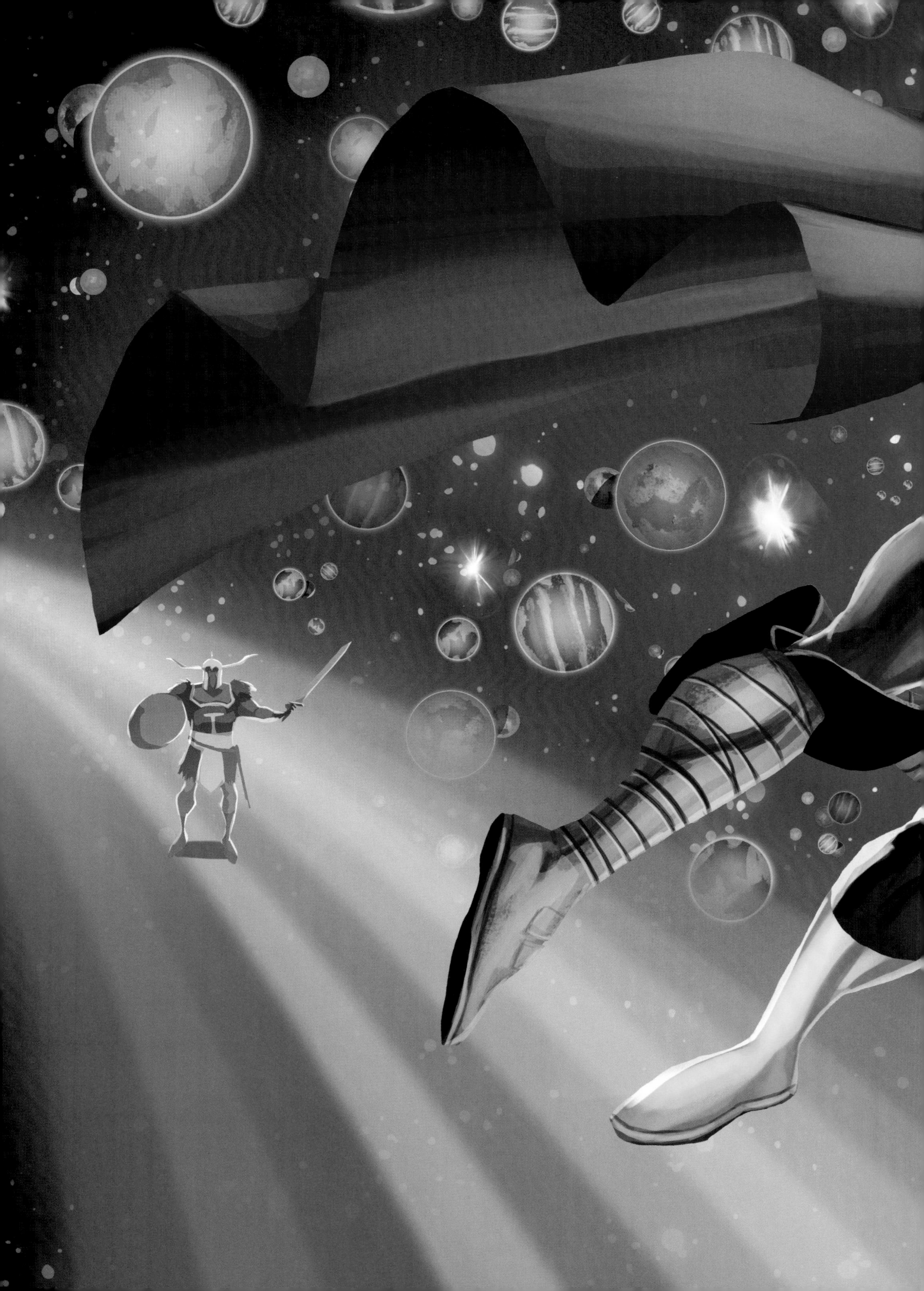

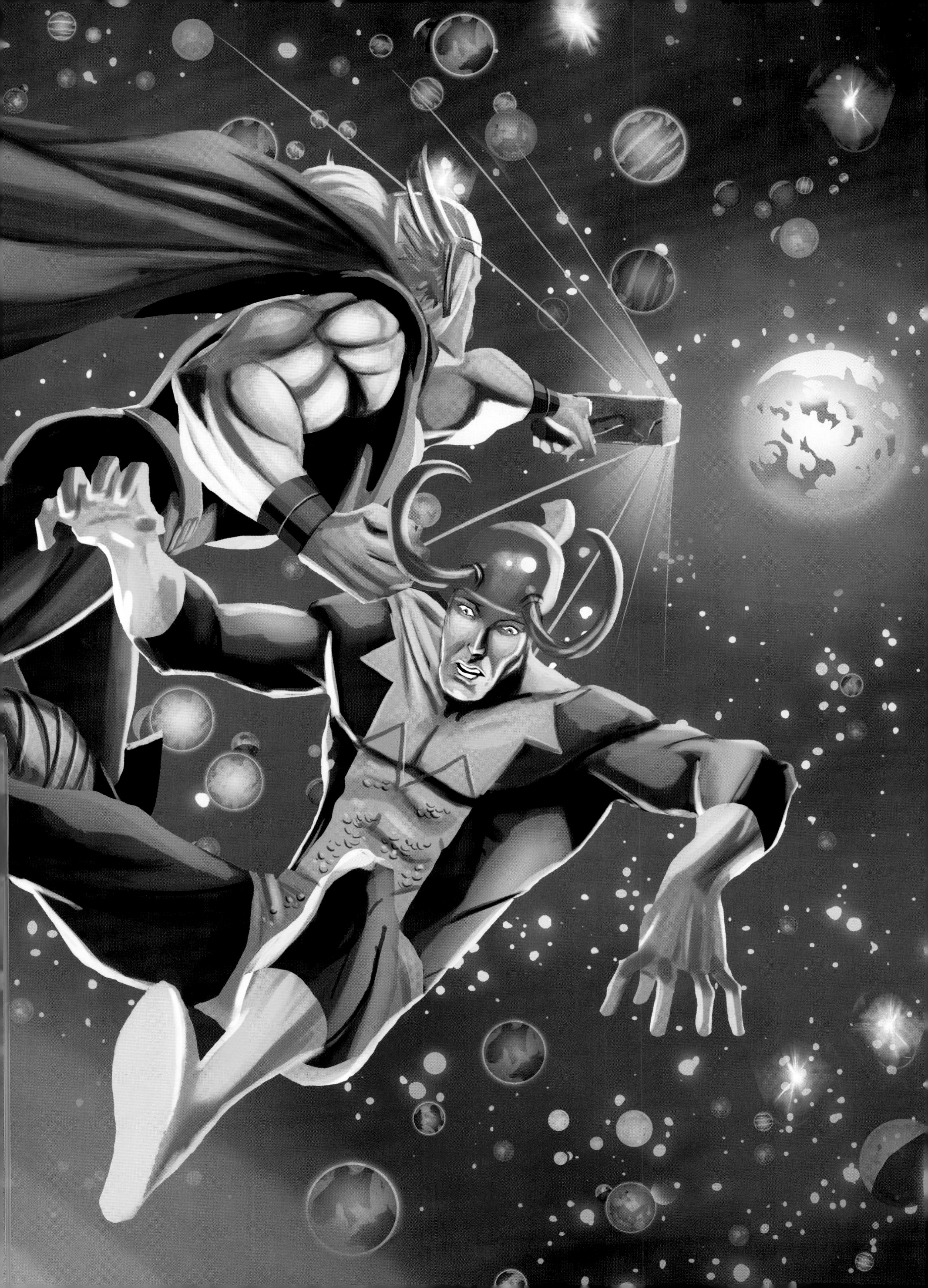

Back on Earth, the battle continued.

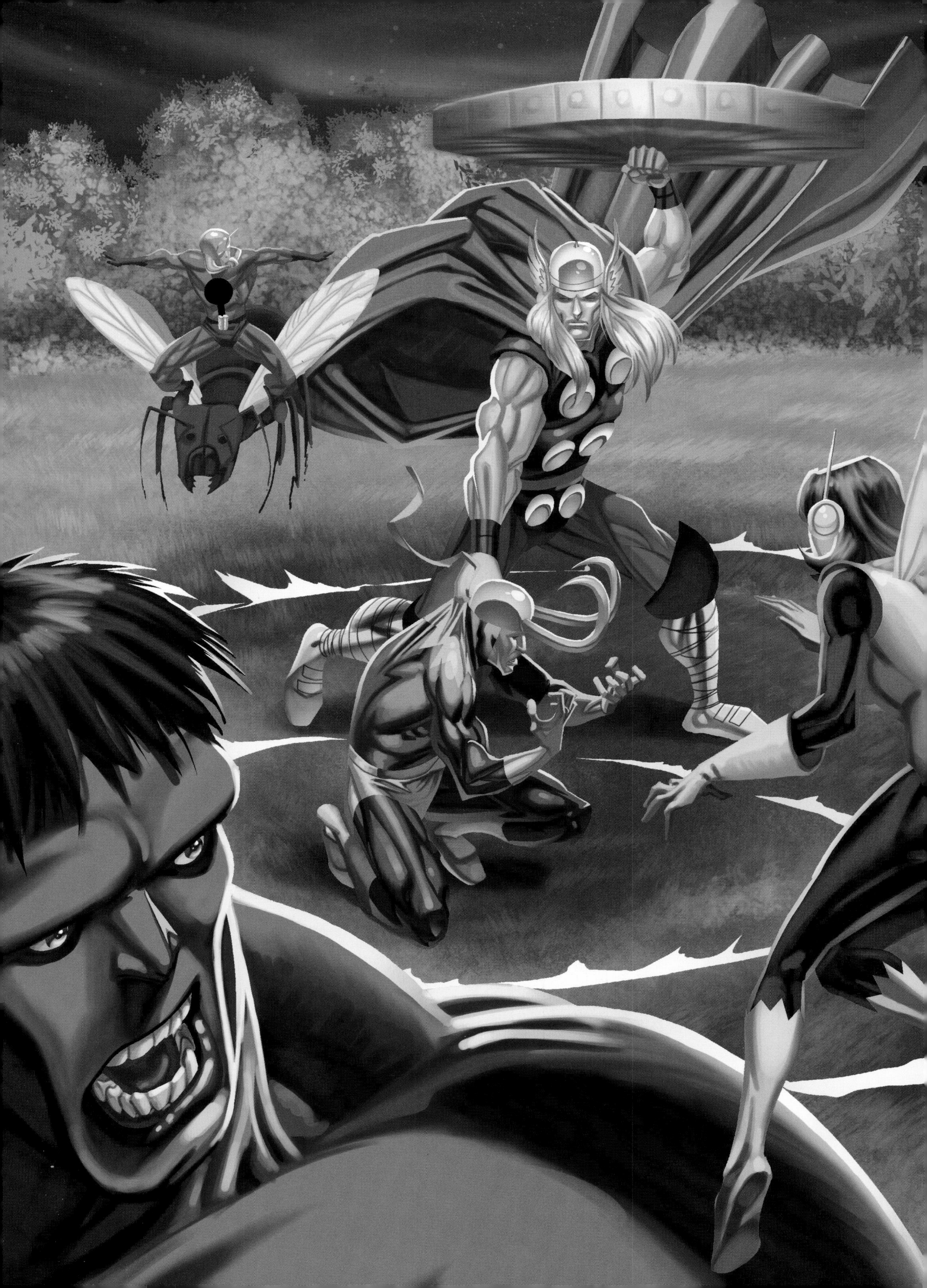

Thor explained that it was **Loki**—not the Hulk—
who had caused all the trouble.

But Loki would not give up.

He used his power to make it seem like there were **many** of him.

But one by one,

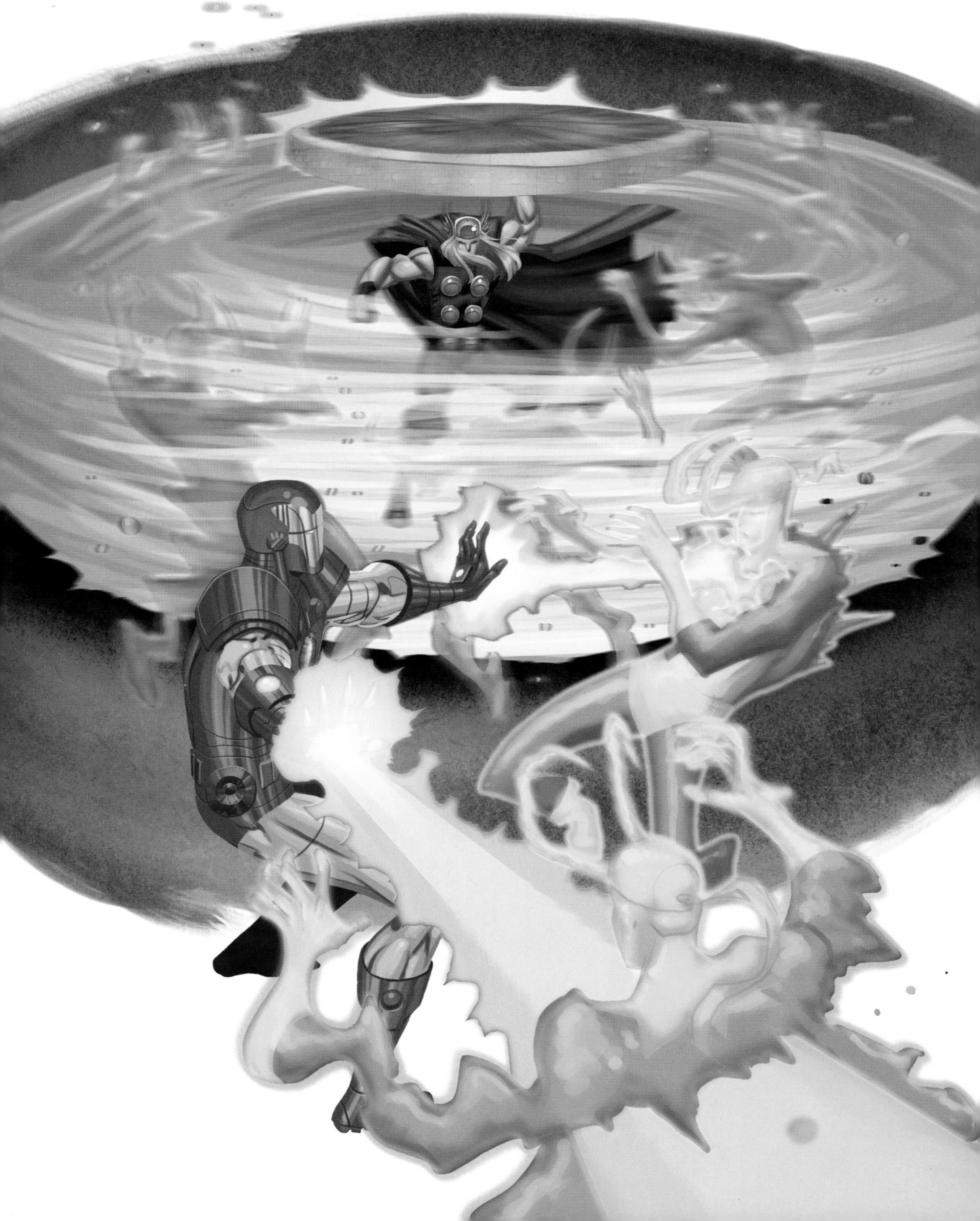

the heroes figured out which
were not the real Loki.

And then one hero discovered the **true villain.**

Loki had been stopped. He would not rule Asgard—
today or ever! But it couldn't have been done by any
one hero alone. The world would forever remember
this as the day a great team was born . . .

. . . and **the Mighty Avengers** first assembled!